BEAR & ALLIGATOR · T·A·L·E·S

When Nicki Went Away

By Fay Robinson
Illustrations by Ann Iosa

CHILDRENS PRESS ®

CHICAGO

Library of Congress Cataloging-in-Publication Data

Robinson, Fay.
    When Nicki went away / by Fay Robinson : illustrated by Ann Iosa.
      p. cm. — (Bear and alligator tales)
    Summary: Nicki's toy animals play and make big messes in different rooms
of the house while the family is away.
    ISBN 0-516-02376-4
    [1. Toys—Fiction. 2. Animals—Fiction.] I. Iosa, Ann, ill. II. Title. III. Series:
Robinson, Fay. Bear and alligator tales.
PZ7.R56564Wh   1992
[E]—dc20   92–13835
                                          CIP
                                          AC

1 2 3 4 5 6 7 8 9 10 R 01 00 99 98 97 96 95 94 93 92

Nicki and her parents were going
to Grandma's.

"Be good," said Nicki. "We will
be gone one week."

4

On Sunday, Alligator played swamp
in the bathroom. The others joined
him.

On Monday, Bear played cave in
the kitchen. The others joined him.

On Tuesday, Pig played pigsty in
the dining room. The others joined her.

12

On Wednesday, Dog played circus
in the living room. The others joined
him.

13

On Thursday, Ape played jungle
in the bedroom. The others joined
him.

On Friday, the house was a huge mess.

"Oh, no! Nicki and her parents will be home tomorrow!" said Bear.

Alligator cleaned up the bathroom.

Bear cleaned up the kitchen.

22

Pig cleaned up the dining room.

Dog cleaned up the living room.

Ape cleaned up the bedroom.

26

They worked all day and all night!

On Saturday, Nicki and her
parents came home. "What good animals
you have been," she said.

About the Author

Fay Robinson received a bachelor's degree in Child Study from Tufts University and a master's degree in Education from Northwestern University. She has taught preschool and elementary children and is the author of several picture books.

About the Artist

Ann Iosa received her professional training at Paier School of Art in New Haven, Connecticut. Her illustrations have appeared in numerous children's books, as well as in several popular magazines. Ann lives with her husband and two children in Southbury, Connecticut.